VIKING
Published by the Penguin Group
Penguin Putnam Inc., 375 Hudson Street, New York, New York 10014, U.S.A.
Penguin Books Ltd., 27 Wrights Lane, London W8 5TZ, England
Penguin Books Australia Ltd, Ringwood, Victoria, Australia
Penguin Books Canada Ltd, 10 Alcorn Avenue, Toronto, Ontario, Canada M4V 3B2
Penguin Books (N.Z.) Ltd, 182–190 Wairau Road, Auckland 10, New Zealand

Penguin Books Ltd, Registered Offices: Harmondsworth, Middlesex, England

First published in 1997 by Anytime Books, a member of Penguin Putnam Inc.

1 3 5 7 9 10 8 6 4 2

Copyright © Nancy Carlson, 1997

ISBN 0–670–78151–7

Printed in U.S.A.

Set in OptiFob

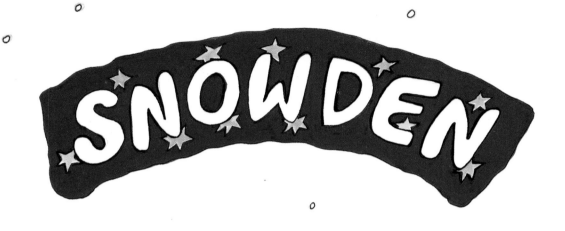

It was a perfect winter's day. Kelly's new friend Sara had invited her to go ice skating.

Kelly was nervous.
Grandpa had taught her how to skate,
but that had been a long time ago.
"I'll make a fool of myself," she thought.

To make matters worse, her mom had bought her a used pair of boy's figure skates.

A girl at the pond skated up to them. "Nice skates," she said, laughing. Kelly felt miserable.

"Ignore Susie, she's just a show-off," said Sara.

Kelly put the skates on. She took one step on the ice and fell flat on her bottom.

"Looks like you need double runners," said Susie.

The next day, Kelly decided not to go skating with Sara.

After a while, Kelly decided to build a snowman.
She used coal, and a parsnip, and Grandpa's old scarf
and hat . But when she put Grandpa's skates around the snowman's
neck, something strange happened. . . .

"Thank you!" said the snowman.
"Wow! Grandpa always called those his magic skates. I guess he was right!" said Kelly. "But who *are* you?"

"I'm Snowden!" said the snowman. "Let's put these skates to use. Want to go skating?" he asked.

"No—I never want to go skating again. The kids all laugh at me," said Kelly. And she went inside.

During dinner, Kelly said, "Um, Mom, what would you say if I told you my snowman was alive?"

Kelly's mom laughed. "I'd say you'd probably spent too much time out in the cold!"

"Ha, ha . . . right," said Kelly.

Later, Kelly went outside to check on Snowden. "You really want to skate, don't you?" she asked him.

Snowden nodded.

"Well . . . no one's there now. Maybe we could go down to the pond for a *little* while," Kelly said.

At the pond, Snowden laced up his skates,
stepped onto the ice, and . . .

"Ouch! I thought you said these were magic skates," said Snowden.
"You're going to need a little magic and a *lot* of practice to be a skater.
Maybe we can help each other," said Kelly.

At first they wobbled a lot, but soon they were skating much better.

It was late when Kelly and Snowden got home, but they promised to skate again the next night.
While Kelly slept, Snowden made some new friends.

**The next night, Snowden brought all of his new friends along.
It was a grand night of skating!**

From then on, Kelly skated with Snowden and their new friends every night. Snowden learned to spin . . .

and Kelly learned to do an axel.

One morning, Kelly decided she was ready to skate with the other kids.
"C'mon, Snowden. Let's go!" she said.
"I can't go down there!" Snowden said. "Someone will call the media,
and reporters will show up with their hot TV lights. . . . I'll melt!"
"I guess you're right," said Kelly sadly.

"But you go ahead, Kelly," said Snowden.
"I can't skate without you!" Kelly said.
"Oh yes you can. You'll show them!" said Snowden.

Kelly spotted Susie as soon as she got to the pond.
"Not you again! Still in those ugly skates, I see," said Susie.
Then Kelly caught sight of her friends peeking through the trees.

Kelly laced up her skates, jumped onto the ice,
and did an axel and a sit spin!

Then she finished with a spiral. Susie was amazed. "How in the world did you learn to skate so well?" she asked.
"Oh, with a little magic and lots of practice," said Kelly.